SARAH WALKER

Ghosts International
Troll and Other Stories

Illustrated by
Paul Fisher-Johnson

OXFORD UNIVERSITY PRESS

UNIVERSITY PRESS

Great Clarendon Street, Oxford, OX2 6DP, United Kingdom

Oxford University Press is a department of the University of Oxford.
It furthers the University's objective of excellence in research, scholarship,
and education by publishing worldwide. Oxford is a registered trade
mark of Oxford University Press in the UK and in certain other countries

© Oxford University Press 2012

The moral rights of the author have been asserted

First published in Oxford Bookworms 2012

10 9 8 7 6 5 4 3 2 1

ISBN: 978 0 19 479386 5

A complete recording of this Bookworms edition of *Ghosts International:
Troll and Other Stories* is also available in an audio pack. ISBN: 978 0 19 479384 1

Printed in China

Word count (main text): 6,808 words

For more information on the Oxford Bookworms Library,
visit www.oup.com/bookworms

OXFORD BOOKWORMS LIBRARY
Fantasy & Horror

Ghosts International
Troll and Other Stories

Stage 2 (700 headwords)

Series Editor: Jennifer Bassett
Founder Editor: Tricia Hedge
Activities Editors: Jennifer Bassett and Christine Lindop

CONTENTS

Troll

A story from Sweden

In Norway, Sweden, Denmark, Finland, and Iceland, people tell many different stories about trolls. Trolls are big, ugly creatures, who live in the mountains . . . Or they are small and horrible, and make trouble around the house. Some stories say you can see them, some say you can only feel that a troll is near.

This story comes from a Swedish woman called Sonja. It is a true story, she says, and it really happened to her.

When I was a little girl, many years ago, I lived with my mother and father and grandfather in my grandfather's house. It was an old house with a big garden, which had a lot of fruit trees in it.

My mother and my father both worked all day, so my grandfather took care of me. I loved my grandfather and I followed him everywhere. When he was working, I liked to watch, and I always tried to help.

One sunny morning after breakfast my grandfather went out into the garden and I went with him. He looked at one of the old apple trees, shook his head, then went back into the house. I followed him. He went to his tool cupboard and began to look through his tools.

At the back of the cupboard was a metal saw, for cutting wood. But now the saw was old and broken.

'Are you going to cut some wood, Grandpa?' I said. 'Can I help you?'

'No, little Sonja,' Grandpa said. 'This old saw is

Grandpa put the broken saw into the tree, high up.

broken now. But it can still do a job, and you can help. I'll need a hammer and some nails too. Please carry the nails for me. I'll carry the hammer because it's heavy.'

Grandpa carried the broken saw and the hammer into the garden. I followed him with the nails. I said to myself, 'I'm helping Grandpa!'

In the garden, Grandpa went to one of the old apple trees. He put the broken saw into the tree, high up. First he made a little cut in the tree, and then pushed the saw hard into the cut. Then he took three nails from me, and hammered them into the tree, around the old saw.

It was a very old tree, and I saw that there were lots of old nails in it.

Grandpa finished. 'There,' he said. 'That's good. The saw won't fall out of the tree now.'

I was only six years old, and I did not understand.

'Grandpa,' I asked. 'Why did you do that?'

'Because of trolls,' Grandpa said.

I knew that a troll was a kind of monster. People said they were ugly and frightening and dangerous, and that they did bad things. But I did not know what things.

'Trolls don't like metal,' said Grandpa. 'If you put something metal in a tree, like that old saw, then the trolls will stay away. They will not come into your garden or into your house while the metal is there.'

He touched the tree, with the old nails in it.

'My father put metal in these trees,' he said, 'and my

grandfather did it before him, and his father before that. And I do the same. Young people today don't follow these ways, but I'm teaching you, little Sonja, so you'll know. And that's why we put that old saw in this tree.'

'What will happen if you don't put something metal in a tree?' I asked.

'If you don't do it, then perhaps a troll will come,' said Grandpa. 'If you are lucky, it will not stay. It will just pass through the garden, maybe. But if you are unlucky – very unlucky – the troll will come into your house. If you are really unlucky, the troll will stay. It will sit in your kitchen. You won't see it, but you will know it is there.'

'If a troll comes and sits in the kitchen, what will it do?' I asked.

Grandpa looked very serious.

'A troll does not need to do anything,' he said. 'Just a troll sitting in your house, in your kitchen! Nothing can be right in a house if a troll is there! Nothing can go right in the family! All the good luck, all the happiness goes out of the house when a troll sits in your kitchen. That is terrible enough!'

After a few years, my mother and father and I left my grandfather's house, and moved into a modern house with a little garden of our own. I forgot about trolls. My mother and father never talked about trolls, and nobody put metal in the trees in our garden.

There were two young trees in the garden and between them there was a washing line. On sunny days we put our wet clothes out on the washing line to get dry.

On my grandfather's first visit, he sat in the kitchen with my mother and father, drinking coffee and talking, and looking out of the window at our garden.

It was a beautiful sunny day. There were wet clothes on the washing line, but they did not move because there was no wind. Everything was still in the garden that day.

My grandfather sat in the kitchen, drinking coffee and talking.

I sat in the kitchen and listened to my grandfather and my parents for a while. But the garden looked so beautiful! I decided to go out and play, and I went to the garden door to go out.

Suddenly my grandfather said, 'Sonja, stop!'

I stopped, with my hand on the door.

Grandpa was looking through the window at the garden outside.

'Troll!' he said. His face was white.

In the garden, the sun was shining. There was no wind. No leaves moved on the trees, everything was still.

But the wet clothes on the washing line were moving, all by themselves. They were turning, and turning – this way, and that way . . .

They were tying themselves into knots.

A Gift for Omar

A story from Oman

All over the world there are stories about meeting strange travellers in lonely places. Who are they? Where have they come from? Where are they going?

This is one of those stories. It happens in Oman, on Route 21, the long road that runs across the lonely hills behind the great Al Hajar mountains.

Oman is a big country, and the roads in Oman are very long. 'Long and empty,' thought Abdul.

He was standing next to his car, by the side of Route 21, the long road that runs from Buraimi to Nizwa. He was waiting for a car to pass by, but the road was empty. There were no houses and no traffic.

Abdul was angry with his car, because it did not go any more. He was angry with himself, because he did not check the car before he left Buraimi. And he was angry with his mobile phone too, because there was no signal. He couldn't use it to phone for help.

Every Wednesday evening, Abdul drove from his office in Buraimi to his family home in Nizwa. He liked to spend the weekend, which in Oman is Thursday and Friday, at home with his family.

He put his hand in his pocket and touched a hard, flat box. It was a computer game – a gift, a present for his youngest brother, Omar. Omar was eight years old and loved computer games. This was a new game, the very newest game. Only one of the computer shops in Buraimi had it, and Abdul was the first person to buy it.

'Omar will be so excited!' he thought. 'He'll have this game before any of his friends have it.'

He bought the game, left Buraimi, and started driving to Nizwa. He wanted to get home before Omar was asleep. So he did not wait to check his car before he left Buraimi, which was a mistake. A big mistake.

Now he was standing by the side of the road, with a dead car, in the middle of nowhere.

'How long will I have to wait before another car comes along?' he thought. 'It's getting dark.'

He looked up at the sky. The sun was down behind the mountains, and the stars were beginning to come out. A hot dry wind was blowing. There was no moon.

At that moment he saw car lights.

'It's my lucky night after all,' he thought. The car was coming very fast over the hills. Its lights looked unusual – very yellow, like the eyes of a cat … or a tiger.

'That's strange,' thought Abdul. Then he saw that the car would be past him in a second. He moved into the road, put both his arms above his head, and waved.

The car made a noise like a scream and stopped right

in front of him. It was a long, black car. Abdul did not know what kind of car it was, but it looked fast.

The door opened and the driver looked out at Abdul. He was wearing dark glasses and had a big smile – a very big smile. Abdul started to say something about his car,

The driver was wearing dark glasses and had a big smile.

about going to Nizwa. The driver did not say anything, but he waved his hand at the seat next to him. Abdul got in and closed the door. The car screamed again and drove quickly away.

Inside the car it was dark and quiet. The only light was a kind of red or orange.

'Where's that light coming from?' thought Abdul. He spoke to the driver, telling him again that he was going to Nizwa.

The driver did not answer. He just smiled his big smile and looked at the road. His glasses were very dark.

'I can't see his eyes behind those glasses, but I think he's looking at the road,' thought Abdul. 'I hope he is. He's driving so fast!'

The driver was wearing a traditional long robe, which hid his legs and feet.

Abdul looked out of the window. The car was moving very fast.

'That's good,' Abdul told himself. 'Fast is good. I'll get home to Nizwa quickly, driving like this. I'll see my family and give Omar his gift, his computer game. This driver's a bit strange – I really don't like that smile! – but it doesn't matter. The important thing is to get home.'

It was night now. The dark road, passing quickly, looked different from usual.

'Where are we?' thought Abdul, looking out of the window again. 'I know this road very well – I drive along it twice a week. Why does it look different tonight?'

Inside the car, the red and orange light looked a little brighter.

'Where's that light coming from?' thought Abdul. 'What is it? It's moving all the time. It looks like . . . it looks like fire. But it can't be. There can't be a fire in here, inside this car.'

He looked at the driver and quickly looked away again. The smile was even bigger than before.

'That smile is horrible,' he thought. 'I don't want to look at it. I'm sure he knows I'm looking at him. But how can he see through those dark glasses? Don't think about it! The important thing is to get home.'

Abdul thought about the big family house in Nizwa, with its big wooden front door. It was safe there.

The thought of home made him feel better. 'Everything will be fine when I get home. I'll open the door and walk in. It will be late, and everyone will be asleep, but I'll see them all in the morning, and I'll give Omar his gift then.'

He put his hand into his pocket and touched the hard flat box of the computer game, the gift for his little brother.

'There it is,' he thought. 'Omar's gift. I hope he likes it.'

'Yes,' said the driver. 'He will enjoy your gift.'

Abdul was very surprised – and afraid. 'What's

happening?' he thought. 'I didn't speak! I was *thinking,* not speaking, but the driver answered my thought. He knows what I'm thinking! He can hear my thoughts.'

He looked at the driver. The driver was looking at the road in front of him, and he was still smiling that big, horrible smile. The light in the car was brighter, more red and orange.

And then Abdul understood. The strange light was coming from the driver – from behind his dark glasses.

'His eyes!' Abdul thought. 'His eyes are made of fire!'

It was only a thought. But Abdul knew now that the driver could hear him. He felt cold with fear. He tried to stop thinking about eyes of fire, about the road which looked different, and about the car which screamed like an animal. He thought about his family, about rain falling on the trees in Nizwa, about playing football with Omar.

The driver's smile got bigger. He turned to look at Abdul, and put his hand up to his dark glasses.

'Oh no!' thought Abdul. 'He's going to take his glasses off!'

Abdul forgot about getting home. He forgot about seeing his family. He even forgot about his little brother Omar, and the gift for him in his pocket. He thought about only one thing.

He did not want to see the driver's eyes!

Abdul put his hand on the car door next to him.

The driver took off his dark glasses. Abdul looked

down, away from the driver's face. The light inside the car suddenly got brighter. It was a moving light, red and orange, like fire. By the strange light, Abdul saw the driver's foot under his long robe.

It was the foot of an animal.

The car door opened suddenly. Abdul fell out.

By the strange light, Abdul saw the driver's foot under his long robe.

When Abdul opened his eyes, he was lying on stones.

He got up carefully. Nothing was broken, but he hurt all over. His face felt dirty and there were little stones in his hair. He looked around quickly. He could not see the long black car, but he still felt afraid.

'Perhaps the driver will come back and find me,' he thought. 'If he comes back . . . What do I do then?'

He looked around again, and for the first time that night, he knew the road. He was near a place called Tanuf, which was not far from Nizwa. He could call a taxi out from Nizwa to take him home.

Home! Abdul stopped feeling afraid. He would soon be home. He put his hand into his pocket and found his mobile phone. There was a good signal, and he called a number in Nizwa and asked for a taxi to take him home. It was late, after midnight.

'They'll all be asleep now,' he thought. 'I won't wake them up. I'll just go in quietly, and see them all in the morning.'

Abdul put his hand in his pocket again. It was empty. The computer game, his gift for Omar, was not there.

Abdul looked for the computer game, walking up and down the road. He moved stones and looked underneath them, but he could not find it anywhere. He was still looking for Omar's gift when the taxi arrived.

In the taxi, Abdul started to feel better. He did not

*Abdul looked for the computer game, walking
up and down the road.*

want to think about the driver, with his horrible smile
and his eyes of fire. He thought about being safe.

'The good thing,' he thought, 'is that he . . . it . . . that
driver, did not take me all the way home. He knows that
I live in Nizwa, but that's all. He doesn't know which

street, and he doesn't know my name. He can't find me, or my family. So I don't need to worry.'

Abdul felt sorry about his brother's present. But Omar was safe. His family was safe. He didn't have a gift for Omar now, but it was not important.

'I can buy another computer game next week,' he thought. 'This weekend I haven't got a gift for him, but it doesn't matter. We'll have a good time. Maybe we'll play football tomorrow. And that thing . . . that creature, with those eyes . . . he can't hurt us. He can't find us.'

It was a long time after midnight when the taxi stopped outside Abdul's home in Nizwa. Abdul paid the driver and walked to the door of his house. Then he stopped.

Outside the door lay a flat, thin box. Abdul knew what it was.

It was the computer game, his gift for Omar.

A New Year's Game

A story from England

'Scrying' is a very old word. It means trying to see into the future. People have tried to do this for hundreds of years, sometimes seriously, sometimes just as a game.

This story is about a scrying game in England in the 1600s. At that time many people believed that scrying was possible – and especially possible by young boys and girls who were not yet married.

*I*t was a cold winter but, inside the big house, the fires burned brightly and the young people kept warm.

There were five of them, all cousins, staying at Great Uncle Edmund's big house. There was Bess and her brother Jack, there was Tom and his sister Joan, and there was Alice. Their parents were all staying in the house too, but they don't come into this story.

The young cousins enjoyed the winter holidays at Great Uncle Edmund's house. They played games, danced, and sang. They went to the village church in the snow. In the evenings they sat around the fire, played games, talked, and told stories until late at night.

Now it was New Year's Eve – December the 31st, the evening of the last day of the old year. Tomorrow was

New Year's Day. Outside it was dark and cold; inside by the fire in the children's room, it was bright and warm.

'What shall we do this evening?' said Joan. She was fourteen, the oldest of the cousins.

'Let's play a game,' Alice said.

'What game?' asked Jack. 'We've played all the games already.' Jack was ten, the youngest and noisiest of the cousins. He and his sister Bess, who was older, were always fighting.

'I know a good game,' said Tom.

'We've played all the games already,' said Jack again.

'We haven't played this one,' said Tom.

'I have,' said Jack.

'Oh, be quiet, Jack!' said his sister Bess. 'Go on, Tom.'

'I read about this game in a book,' said Tom. He was twelve, a clever boy, who always had his head in a book. 'You can only do this on one night of the year. Just tonight – New Year's Eve.'

'Oooh!' said Bess. 'You mean scrying. Oh, let's do it!'

'What's scrying?' asked Alice.

'Scrying is a way of seeing the future,' said Bess.

'That sounds exciting!' said Jack. 'How do you do it?'

'Don't you need to look into a mirror?' asked Joan.

'No,' said Tom. 'This is what you do. You go to the church at midnight on New Year's Eve. You wait outside the church door, and watch. That's all.'

'Yes, I remember now,' said Joan. 'It happens between

'I read about this game in a book,' said Tom.

the old year and the New Year, when the church clock
strikes twelve midnight.'

'What happens then?' asked Alice. She was a quiet
child, with soft brown eyes. She was not sure she wanted
to know about scrying.

'You scry – you see things,' said Tom. 'That's all.'

'What . . . what kind of things?' said Alice.

The village had a big churchyard which went all round
the church. Alice did not want to go there at night. All
those dead bodies lying under the ground, she thought.
Hundreds of them, men and women and children.
Everyone who died in the village was lying there.

'Do . . . do you mean ghosts? Do the ghosts of the
dead come out of the ground?' she asked.

Jack liked to frighten girls. 'Oooooh, ghosts! Monsters
with no eyes!'

'No, not ghosts,' said Bess. 'Stop it, Jack!'

'Don't listen to Jack, Alice,' said Joan. 'It isn't ghosts
or monsters, Tom, is it?'

'Of course not,' said Tom. 'You just see all the people
who are going to die in the next year. Well, that's what
the books say. I've never tried it.'

'All the people in England?' said Alice. 'That will take
hours! It will take all night!'

'Of course not,' said Joan. 'It's just people from this
village, I think. Anyone who will lie in the churchyard
after they die, that's all.'

'That's right,' said Tom. 'They walk through the churchyard, past the church door.'

'Are they . . . are they dangerous?' asked Alice.

'Yes,' said Jack. 'They'll catch you and drink your blood!'

'Stop it!' said Bess and Joan together. Bess gave her brother a push in the back. 'You're horrible!' she said.

'They're not ghosts, because they're not dead yet,' said Tom. 'They're just people who are going to die in the next year. Right now, they're really at home, asleep, or sitting by the fire. You just see them, that's all. It's like looking at a picture, I think. That's what scrying is, really, seeing pictures of the future.'

Alice thought about this. 'What happens,' she asked, 'if you see someone from your family?'

'She's afraid!' said Jack. 'I'm not! I'll go. It's exciting.'

'But what happens,' Alice went on, 'if you see your mother or your father in the churchyard? I think it's a horrible game!'

'Listen,' said Joan. 'Your parents aren't ill, are they?'

'No. They're very well, thank you.'

'And my parents are fine,' said Tom, 'and so are Bess and Jack's parents. And Great Uncle Edmund plans to live until he's a hundred. He told me that.'

Bess laughed. 'You see, Alice, there's no need to worry. Nobody in the family is ill, and if they aren't ill, they aren't going to die, are they?'

*'What happens,' Alice asked, 'if you see
someone from your family?'*

'No,' said Alice. She felt Tom and Bess were wrong,
but she did not know why.

'Well,' said Bess, 'I'm going to go scrying.'

'I'll go if you go,' said Joan.

'I'm going!' said Jack. 'I'm not afraid.'

'You don't have to come, Alice,' said Joan. 'You
can stay here if you're frightened. Go and sit with the
parents round the fire in the hall. We'll go without you.'

'Yes,' said Tom. 'But you mustn't tell anybody that

we've gone out. Don't say anything about scrying!'

Alice looked at her cousins. It was her first holiday with them. She liked them very much, and she wanted them to like her. She thought about sitting in the hall with the noisy adults, saying nothing, waiting for the sound of the church clock at midnight, waiting for her cousins to come back.

'Perhaps they won't come back,' she thought. 'Perhaps they will see something really horrible in the churchyard.' Alice's heart gave a little jump when she thought this.

She did not want to go scrying, but she wanted to be with her cousins.

'All right,' she said. 'I'll come scrying with you.'

'Hooray!' said Jack.

'Good,' said Joan.

'We'll take care of you, Alice,' said Tom.

'All right,' said Alice. 'I'm . . . I'm not afraid really.'

'What about our parents?' asked Bess. 'Will they stop us going out to the churchyard?'

'We're not going to tell them!' said Joan.

'They're all in the great hall, and they're making a lot of noise,' Tom said. 'If we go downstairs quietly, they won't hear us.'

Soon they heard the church clock. It struck eleven times – eleven o'clock. Alice looked out of the window. There was no wind. Everything was quiet. She could see the church through the trees. Snow lay deep on the ground in the churchyard around the church. The room was warm, but Alice suddenly felt cold.

Time passed quickly, and very soon Tom said, 'Time to get ready. Let's go!'

The five young people put on warm clothes and winter boots. They went quietly downstairs, and quickly past the door of the great hall. There was a lot of noisy laughing, and someone was singing a song very loudly.

'That's Great Uncle Edmund singing,' whispered Joan. 'Mother says he will sing all night if nobody stops him.'

Tom softly opened the big front door, and the five of them went outside. It was dark and cold. Jack carried a lamp, but the light was not very strong.

Nothing moved in the still, white night – only the five young people. They walked quietly through the snow to the church. Their feet made a noise on the snow, crunch, crunch, crunch. It was the only sound.

They went through the churchyard to the church door. There were seats on each side of the door, and the five young people sat together on one seat. They sat close together because it was so cold.

Alice was at one end, next to the big wooden door of the church. Her hands and her feet felt very cold, and her heart was jumping, but she was not afraid any more. She felt that she was waiting for something very important. The future was very close. Soon she would see it.

'Jack was right,' she thought. 'This is exciting!'

*The five young people walked quietly through the snow
to the church.*

All five sat looking out at the quiet churchyard. They saw only the dark trees and the white snow. Nothing moved. Nobody spoke.

BONG!

The loud noise made them all jump. Alice gave a little scream. Joan screamed too, and then laughed.

The church clock was striking. It was twelve o'clock, midnight. The old year was ending.

'It's now,' said Tom, 'while the clock is striking. That's when it happens.'

BONG!

'Look!' whispered Joan.

Something was moving on the other side of the churchyard. It was coming slowly through the trees to the church. It came closer. They could not hear a sound. It was a man – an old man, walking slowly. But his feet left no footprints in the snow.

'Who is it?' said Jack. His voice was unusually quiet.

'It's . . . it's old Mr Jenkins,' said Bess. 'Mother said he was ill. I think that means . . .'

'It means he's going to die this year,' said Tom, very quietly.

BONG! went the church clock.

The old man crossed the churchyard slowly and walked on past the church door. He did not look at the young people.

BONG!

Another person was now coming through the churchyard. It was a very old woman. She came through the trees and crossed the churchyard slowly. They all knew her. It was Lady Hampton, who lived in a big house in the village.

The old man's feet left no footprints in the snow.

BONG!

Lady Hampton moved silently away over the snow.

Behind Lady Hampton came a young woman.

'Oh!' said Jack, 'I know who that is. It's Mrs White.'

'Oh no!' said Joan. 'That's terrible! She's young!'

'She only got married last spring,' said Bess. 'Poor Mr White! How sad he'll be!'

The young woman was carrying something in her arms.

'What's she holding?' whispered Tom.

BONG!

'It looks like a baby,' said Joan.

'That's impossible. She hasn't got a baby,' said Jack.

'No,' said Bess, 'but Mother says she's going to have one.'

BONG!

Mrs White carried her baby past the church door. Joan turned her head away. She did not want to see the baby in Mrs White's arms.

Another person, someone small, was now moving silently over the snow.

BONG!

'Who is it?' said Jack.

'I'm not sure,' said Bess. 'Someone . . . someone young.'

'It's a girl,' said Tom.

BONG!

The girl came closer.

'It looks like . . .' began Joan.

BONG!

It was Alice.

Joan screamed. They all turned to their cousin. She was still sitting on the seat next to the church door. Her eyes were open, but she was looking at nothing. Bess took Alice's hand and Joan shook her. They tried to wake her, but they could not. Her hand and her face were cold. She was not breathing.

BONG!

They turned back to the churchyard. The young girl was moving slowly away across the snowy churchyard. She looked neither to right nor left, and made no sound.

Jack ran. His feet crunched on the snow. He put out his hand to touch her, but at the same moment, his foot hit something. He fell, crying, into the snow.

BONG!

She was gone.

Bess and Jack, Tom and Joan, were alone in the churchyard with their young cousin. Alice was dead.

A few days later, Alice's body was laid to rest in the churchyard. Snow was still lying on the ground. Most of the village was there – Lady Hampton, and old Mr Jenkins, who already looked ill. It was the cold weather, he said.

Mr White was there too, but his wife stayed at home. He spoke to Alice's parents.

'I'm sorry my wife can't be here,' he said. 'We are both so sorry about your daughter. My wife wanted to come, but she's very tired these days. She'll feel better after the baby is born . . . I'm sure she will.'

The Road Home

A story from East Asia

There have been so many wars, in every country of the world. When the wars finish, the soldiers have to return home. But they are different men, and they return to a different world. War changes people.

This story is about a soldier from East Asia. War has changed him greatly. It is a sad story, but in a strange way, also a happy one.

The long war was over, and the soldier was going home. His road home was long and hard.

In the beginning, the soldier was not alone on the road. Many other soldiers were going home too, and for a long time they walked together, not speaking, just thinking about their homes at the end of the long road.

They walked across rice fields, past banana farms, along empty roads, through silent villages. No lights showed in the windows of the dark houses. Nothing moved, only the soldiers and the wind in the trees.

After a while, each man took his own road home. One turned right and went up into the mountains. Another turned left, down to the sea and the fishing boats. Some soldiers followed the road to far cities; others followed

One by one, they went their different ways.

the small roads into the hills. One by one, they went
their different ways.

The soldier walked on alone, taking his own road
home. He did not think about the other soldiers, or
about the war. He thought only about the long road
back to his home.

'Home,' thought the soldier. 'I know my home is at
the end of this road. I just need to go on walking.'

The road felt hard under his boots, and the only sound was the noise of his boots on the road – tramp, tramp, tramp. He was tired and thirsty, and his mouth was dry as dust.

'There's no water,' he thought. 'Just dust. Dust in my mouth. Dust everywhere.'

Tramp, tramp, tramp went his boots.

'Don't stop walking,' he told himself. 'I can't stop. I mustn't stop. I'll rest when I get home. Mother will make tea, and then I can rest.'

He tried to walk faster, but he felt so tired, so tired. His feet felt heavier and heavier, and he walked more and more slowly. He wanted to lie down by the side of the road, in the dark, and stay there.

'If I lie down,' he thought, 'I'll never get up again.'

So he went on walking, one foot in front of the other, tramp, tramp, tramp.

'The war is finished,' he told himself. 'Forget the war. Just think about home. I must get home. I promised.'

The road began to go up into the hills. There were trees on each side, and their dark leaves in the night made the road dark too. The road climbed up and up into the hills. He knew his home was somewhere on the other side of the hills.

'I can see it now,' he thought. 'Our little house, so small, but always clean and quiet. I can see the lamp on the table . . . I can see Mother, with her long black hair.

She's sitting in her chair, singing my little sister to sleep. My little sister . . . She was just a baby when I left. How old is she now? Three? Four? Can she talk yet?'

He felt sad, because he could not remember his little sister's face.

'But I remember Mother at the door when I went away to the war,' he thought. 'I remember her words, every one of them. *Go safely, and be sure to come back to me.* And I promised her. *I will come home.* Those were my words, and I must keep my promise to her.'

Now the road began to turn downhill, and the land beside the road fell away into fields and woods.

'I know those fields down there,' he thought. 'I know these woods. I can't remember their names, but I know my village is down in this valley. Mother's waiting, down there, at home.'

The soldier walked on, along the dark road under the trees. He was so tired. His feet felt so heavy and his mouth was so dry. He wanted to lie down in the dark and never move again. But his boots went on hitting the road – tramp, tramp, tramp.

'If I stop now,' he told himself, 'I'll never see Mother again. And I promised her, so I must go on walking. Rest. When I get home, I can rest. Mother will make tea. We'll sit in her quiet room and drink tea together, and then my mouth will not be so dry.'

The soldier's village looked different in the dark.

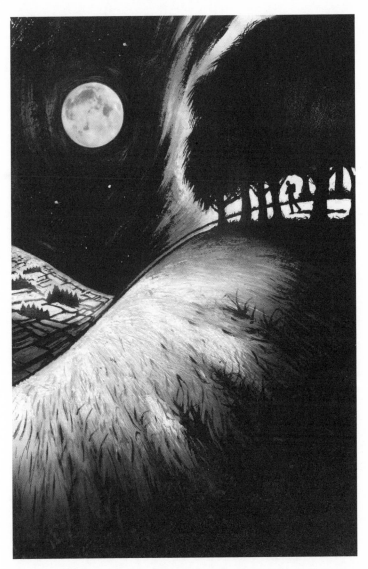

The soldier walked on, along the dark road under the trees.

There were fewer trees and gardens. There were more houses, and they looked bigger than he remembered. But the soldier knew that this was his village at last, at the end of his road. He was nearly home, and home is home.

The soldier went through his village like the wind. In no time at all, he stood outside his mother's little house. It was the smallest house in the village, and the only one that still looked the same. But the soldier did not care about the other houses.

He stood outside his mother's door. He touched the door with his hand, and it opened. Inside he saw the little clean room, the table, the lamp . . . Across the room his mother was lying in her bed.

'Of course,' he thought, 'It's the middle of the night. She's sleeping, of course. She works so hard. She needs to rest, like me.'

Then, for a second, the soldier thought he was in the wrong house, because the body lying in the bed was an old, old woman with white hair.

But at that moment, the body moved. His mother's eyes opened, and she looked at him and smiled. She got up and came across the room to the open door, and took his hand. Something was still lying in the bed behind her, but the soldier looked only at his mother. Still young, with her long dark hair falling around her face.

'I knew you would come back,' she said, 'I waited for you.'

'I came as fast as I could,' said the soldier, 'but it was a long road home.'

'Yes,' said his mother, 'I've waited a long time. But you are home now, at last. Sit down and rest. I will make tea.'

She came across the room to the open door, and took his hand.

The soldier sat down. His mother lit the lamp and made tea, moving quietly around the room. The soldier forgot about the war, and the long road home. He felt quiet and peaceful. His mother put the tea on the table, and they both drank.

The soldier finished his tea. He said, 'I'm sorry it took so long to come home.'

'The important thing is that you have come,' said his mother. 'I've waited a long time for you. So long! But I knew you would come back in the end.'

'I promised you that I would come home,' he said.

'Yes,' said his mother. 'I knew you would keep your promise, and so I waited for you. Now you have come, we can leave together.'

They stood up. The soldier did not feel tired any more. He felt light, like a bird, like a drop of rain. He looked around his mother's room for the last time, then took his mother's hand. Behind them, on the other side of the room, there was something lying in the bed. It was the body of an old, old woman, lying very still. But the soldier did not look at it. He saw only the kind and loving face of his mother, with her long dark hair falling around her face.

The soldier and his mother moved quickly to the door, holding hands. They went outside into the bright starlight, and were gone.

The soldier's little sister visited her mother every day. The sister was now a woman of sixty-eight years, with three adult children of her own, and five grandchildren. Her oldest granddaughter, who was fifteen, was with her today.

The sister lived in a new, modern house just outside the city. She wanted her old mother to come and live with her, in her comfortable modern house, but the mother always said no, she would not leave her little old house. She wanted to stay in her own home.

'Why won't she come and live with us, Grandma?' asked the sister's granddaughter.

'It's because of my brother,' said the sister. 'Years ago, when I was only a baby, there was a war. My brother was a soldier. He went away to the war, and he never came home again.'

'What happened to him?' asked the granddaughter. 'Did he die?'

'I don't know,' said the sister. 'My mother never heard what happened to him. I can't remember him at all, but my mother has never forgotten him. I don't think that a day goes past when she doesn't think about him.'

So many young men went away to that war. So many did not come back. The ones who did come back were now old men, but the soldier's mother went on waiting. She would not move to a new house. Even now, when she was so old herself, she would not leave.

For the last few years, she could not get out of bed.
She was not ill, but she was very tired, and she could not
walk. So the sister came every day to visit her mother
and to sit with her in the little house. A nurse came every
day too, because the mother was so old.

Today, the sister was taking her granddaughter with
her. 'It'll be good for you,' she told her granddaughter,
'to spend some time with my mother.'

'What will we have to do for her, Grandma?' asked the
granddaughter.

'We'll help her sit up in bed,' said the sister. 'We'll
wash her face and tidy her hair. And we'll make tea for
her. When the nurse comes, we can leave.'

They were driving to the mother's house along the
new road. This was a fast road that went from the city
around the hills to the villages in the valley on the other
side. The old road went over the hills.

'You never use the old road, do you, Grandma?' the
granddaughter said.

'No, it takes too long that way,' said the sister.

'Good,' said the granddaughter. 'I don't like that
road. There are lots of trees along it, and they make the
road very dark. Girls at school say that if you walk there
at night, you can hear a ghost.'

The sister laughed. 'A ghost!' she said.

'It's true, Grandma!' said the granddaughter. 'That's
what they say. No one's ever seen the ghost, but people

have heard it. It's someone in heavy boots walking along the road – tramp, tramp, tramp.'

'Ah yes, I remember now,' said the sister. 'There is a story about the road over the hills. When I was a girl at school, years ago, people were telling the same story even then. Some ghost stories go on for ever, don't they?'

'They say that if you walk there at night, you can hear a ghost.'

When they arrived in the village, the sister stopped the car outside her mother's little house. She opened the front door and looked inside. She was not surprised by what she saw.

'Wait outside,' she told her granddaughter quickly. 'Use your mobile phone to call an ambulance. Then wait in the car.' She did not say that a doctor was no longer necessary.

The sister shut the door and sat down next to her mother's bed. She held her mother's cold hand. Her mother looked peaceful, the sister thought. She looked happy.

There was only one thing that the sister did not understand. On the little table, on the other side of the room, there were two empty tea cups.

GLOSSARY

believe   to feel sure that something is true

blow (*v*)   when air or wind blows, it moves

boot   a shoe that covers your foot and sometimes part of your leg

breathe   to take in and let out air through your nose and mouth

broken (*adj*)   in pieces or not working

check   to look at something to see that it is right, good, or safe

churchyard   a piece of land around a church, often used for burying dead people

close (*adj*)   near

cousin   the child of your aunt or uncle

creature   any living thing that is not a plant

crunch   to make a loud noise, e.g., like walking through snow

dust   dry dirt that is like powder

fear   the feeling that you have when you are afraid

footprint   a mark made on the ground by a foot or a shoe

frightening   making you feel afraid

future   the time that will come

game   an activity that you do to have fun

ghost   the form of a dead person that a living person thinks they see

gift   something that you give to somebody, a present

glasses   people wear glasses to help them see better; dark glasses (or sunglasses) have dark glass to protect against sunshine

hammer   a tool with a heavy metal head, used for hitting nails

heart   the part of the body that makes the blood go round inside

horrible   bad or unpleasant

knot   a place where two ends of cloth or string are tied together

lamp   a thing that uses electricity, gas, or oil to produce light

line   a long piece of plastic or rope, for hanging wet washing

metal a hard, solid material, e.g. tin, iron, gold, steel. etc.

mirror a piece of special glass where you can see yourself

monster a creature in stories that is big, ugly, and frightening

nail a small thin piece of metal with a sharp end, used to fix
  things together

peaceful calm and quiet

promise to say that you will certainly do or not do something

robe a long loose piece of clothing

sad unhappy

safe free from danger

saw *(n)* a metal tool for cutting wood

serious not funny, not joking or playing

shine to give out light

signal the radio waves that make mobile phones work

strike (of a clock) to ring a bell a certain number of times so
  that people know what time it is

thought *(n)* thinking; an idea

tie (*present participle* **tying**) to make a knot in something

tiger a large wild cat, with yellow fur and black stripes

tool a thing you hold in your hand and use to do a special job

traditional something that people in a certain place have done
  for a long time

tramp to walk with slow heavy steps, for a long time

troll (in stories) a creature that looks like an ugly person

ugly not pleasant to look at; the opposite of beautiful

valley the low land between mountains

war fighting between countries or between groups of people

wave *(v)* to move your hand from side to side in the air

whisper to speak very quietly

Ghosts International
Troll and Other Stories

ACTIVITIES

ACTIVITIES

Before Reading

1 Read the introduction on the first page of the book, and the back cover. How much do you know now about the stories? Tick one box for each sentence.

	YES	NO
1 There is a ghost or monster in every story.	☐	☐
2 One of the stories happens in the future.	☐	☐
3 In one story a soldier goes away to war.	☐	☐
4 All the stories come from different countries.	☐	☐
5 Sonja's grandfather was a troll.	☐	☐
6 Some people believe in ghosts.	☐	☐
7 Science can explain everything that happens.	☐	☐

2 What can you guess about these stories? Read these sentences, and put a circle round the words that you like best.

1 Sonja's grandfather *hates / likes* trolls.

2 Sonja *sees / does not see* a troll in her garden.

3 Abdul has a *frightening / wonderful* ride with a stranger.

4 Abdul *loses / forgets* the computer game for his little brother Omar.

5 After the 'scrying' game the children are *happy / sorry*.

6 The soldier *finds / does not find* his mother at home.

ACTIVITIES

After Reading

1 **Here are the thoughts of four characters (one from each story). Who is thinking, and in which story? Who are they thinking about, and what is happening in the story?**

   1 'Why can't I stay up a bit later? I'm not at all sleepy! I *did* want to see him – why hasn't he come? He always brings me a gift, and there's that new computer game that all my friends are talking about. Perhaps he's bringing it . . .'

   2 'It's a long time to wait, a very long time. One day soon I'll go to sleep, and never wake up. But I know he'll come back – he promised. He'll come through the door, and I'll make tea for him, the way I always did. That's why I must stay here, in this house, ready for his return . . .'

   3 'Oh no! What have we done? Look at her – she's so white and cold! It was only a game. I feel terrible – it was my idea to try it. Oh, why didn't we stay at home by the fire? We must get help . . . must run back to the house . . .'

   4 'Well, that's a good job done – it'll keep them away. And it's good that my granddaughter helped me. She needs to learn about life's dangers. My son and his wife just laugh, and say they don't believe in these things, but they haven't seen what I've seen . . .'

2 Use the clues to complete this crossword with words from
the stories. All the words go across. When the crossword is
complete, there will be a seven-letter word hidden in the
crossword.

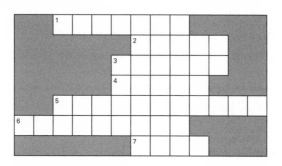

1 The soldier was _____, but there was no water to drink.
2 While the children were watching the churchyard, the
church _____ struck midnight.
3 Sonja's parents don't believe in _____.
4 The wet clothes on the washing line were _____
themselves into knots.
5 The driver of the black car was wearing a _____ robe.
6 The old woman's family called an _____ to the house.
7 Abdul bought a computer _____ for his little brother.

Now find the hidden seven-letter word in the crossword.

1 What is the hidden word?
2 Which story does the word come from?
3 What does the word mean?

3 Match these parts of sentences about the people in the stories. There are three parts to each sentence. Then choose the best linking words to join the parts together.

First parts of the sentence

1 Sonja's grandfather puts something metal in a tree, . . .

2 The soldier wants to see his mother, . . .

3 Alice doesn't want to go scrying, . . .

4 Abdul doesn't check his car . . .

Second parts of the sentence

5 *and / but* she agrees to go, . . .

6 *while / before* he leaves Buraimi, . . .

7 *why / because* he doesn't want a troll in his garden, . . .

8 *which / who* will make tea for him, . . .

Third parts of the sentence

9 *after / before* he gets home.

10 *but / what* Sonja's parents don't do that.

11 *when / so* he has to get in the stranger's car.

12 *because / so* she likes being with her cousins.

4 *A New Year's Game.* Talk about these questions.

1 Would you like to see into the future? Why, or why not?

2 Why is the future so interesting to many people?

3 Is it better to try to enjoy the present, instead of wondering about the future? What is your opinion?

5 *A Gift for Omar.* **What do you think happens next in this story? Answer these questions. Then, using your answers and your own ideas, write a new paragraph to end the story.**

1 What does Abdul do with the computer game? He . . .

   a) throws it away.   c) gives it to Omar.

   b) takes it back to the shop.   d) burns it.

2 What happens with the driver of the black car?

   a) Nobody ever sees him again.

   b) He drives behind Abdul all the way back to Buraimi.

   c) He appears on the screen in the computer game.

   d) He waits in his car outside Abdul's family's house.

6 *Troll.* **When Sonja was much older, she talked to her friend Karin about the troll in her garden. Their conversation is in the wrong order. Put it in the right order and add the speakers' names. Karin speaks first (number 5).**

1 _____ 'Of course there was a wind!'

2 _____ 'Well, I didn't actually *see* one, but the clothes blew about on the washing line!'

3 _____ 'Come on, Sonja! No one believes that kind of thing any more!'

4 _____ 'But there wasn't any wind at all that day!'

5 _____ 'You say you saw a troll in the garden?'

6 _____ 'No, really, there wasn't. The troll was doing it – he was tying the clothes into knots!'

7 _____ 'That's what clothes do when it's windy!'

7 *The Road Home.* Here is a page from the granddaughter's diary some months after the old woman's death. Choose one suitable word to fill each gap.

Today I went back to Great-Grandma's _____. The people there told me something _____. They don't hear the ghostly boots _____ along the road any more. Even _____, they all agree the ghostly sounds _____ suddenly, the day after my poor _____ death! None of us can really _____ it.

8 Look at these possible new titles for the four stories. Match all the titles with the stories. Which one do you like best for each story? Explain why.

Keeping a promise   The Man in Dark Glasses
Route 21   The Washing Line
The Saw in the Tree   The Clock Strikes Midnight
Pictures of the Future   Two Cups of Tea

9 What did you think of the stories? Use the table below to make sentences about them. Use as many words as you like to finish the sentences.

Troll		a bit scary	
A Gift for Omar		very frightening	when . . .
	was	sad	
A New Year's Game		nice	because . . .
The Road Home		exciting	

ABOUT THE AUTHOR

Sarah Walker is a writer, storyteller, and teacher. She was born in London, studied at the University of Birmingham, and then became an English teacher. She has taught students from around the world in the UK, and has also taught in Italy, Spain, Thailand, Laos, the United Arab Emirates, Romania, and China. She has collected stories from many countries, and finds that most people enjoy hearing and telling tales that are just a little bit scary. She now lives in Norwich, in the east of England, and teaches at the University of East Anglia.

The idea for *A New Year's Game* came from a sentence in a book written in the 17th century by a writer called John Aubrey. John Aubrey tells how, when he was young, some young people from his village went to the church on New Year's Eve to try and see the future. This is usually a bad idea!

Many countries have stories about strange meetings on lonely roads. *A Gift for Omar* is set on the long road that runs through the desert from Buraimi on the UAE border to the beautiful town of Nizwa, in Oman.

East Asia, like many other parts of the world, has stories about ghostly soldiers. In *The Road Home* the soldier is trying to return home to the places and the people that he loved.

Troll was collected in Sweden by Sarah's husband, Barrie de Lara. It was told to him by the painter Sigi Boseley ('Sonja' in the story). 'Sonja' told Barrie that it was a true story, and that it really happened to her.

OXFORD BOOKWORMS LIBRARY

Classics • Crime & Mystery • Factfiles • Fantasy & Horror
Human Interest • Playscripts • Thriller & Adventure
True Stories • World Stories

The OXFORD BOOKWORMS LIBRARY provides enjoyable reading in English, with a wide range of classic and modern fiction, non-fiction, and plays. It includes original and adapted texts in seven carefully graded language stages, which take learners from beginner to advanced level. An overview is given on the next pages.

All Stage 1 titles are available as audio recordings, as well as over eighty other titles from Starter to Stage 6. All Starters and many titles at Stages 1 to 4 are specially recommended for younger learners. Every Bookworm is illustrated, and Starters and Factfiles have full-colour illustrations.

The OXFORD BOOKWORMS LIBRARY also offers extensive support. Each book contains an introduction to the story, notes about the author, a glossary, and activities. Additional resources include tests and worksheets, and answers for these and for the activities in the books. There is advice on running a class library, using audio recordings, and the many ways of using Oxford Bookworms in reading programmes. Resource materials are available on the website <www.oup.com/bookworms>.

The *Oxford Bookworms Collection* is a series for advanced learners. It consists of volumes of short stories by well-known authors, both classic and modern. Texts are not abridged or adapted in any way, but carefully selected to be accessible to the advanced student.

You can find details and a full list of titles in the *Oxford Bookworms Library Catalogue* and *Oxford English Language Teaching Catalogues*, and on the website <www.oup.com/bookworms>.

THE OXFORD BOOKWORMS LIBRARY
GRADING AND SAMPLE EXTRACTS

STARTER • 250 HEADWORDS

present simple – present continuous – imperative –
can/cannot, must – going to (future) – simple gerunds ...

Her phone is ringing – but where is it?

Sally gets out of bed and looks in her bag. No phone. She looks under the bed. No phone. Then she looks behind the door. There is her phone. Sally picks up her phone and answers it. *Sally's Phone*

STAGE 1 • 400 HEADWORDS

... past simple – coordination with *and, but, or* –
subordination with *before, after, when, because, so* ...

I knew him in Persia. He was a famous builder and I worked with him there. For a time I was his friend, but not for long. When he came to Paris, I came after him – I wanted to watch him. He was a very clever, very dangerous man. *The Phantom of the Opera*

STAGE 2 • 700 HEADWORDS

... present perfect – *will* (future) – (*don't*) *have to, must not, could* –
comparison of adjectives – simple *if* clauses – past continuous –
tag questions – *ask/tell* + infinitive ...

While I was writing these words in my diary, I decided what to do. I must try to escape. I shall try to get down the wall outside. The window is high above the ground, but I have to try. I shall take some of the gold with me – if I escape, perhaps it will be helpful later. *Dracula*

STAGE 3 • 1000 HEADWORDS
... should, may – present perfect continuous – *used to* – past perfect –
causative – relative clauses – indirect statements ...

Of course, it was most important that no one should see
Colin, Mary, or Dickon entering the secret garden. So Colin
gave orders to the gardeners that they must all keep away
from that part of the garden in future. *The Secret Garden*

STAGE 4 • 1400 HEADWORDS
... past perfect continuous – passive (simple forms) –
would conditional clauses – indirect questions –
relatives with *where/when* – gerunds after prepositions/phrases ...

I was glad. Now Hyde could not show his face to the world
again. If he did, every honest man in London would be proud
to report him to the police. *Dr Jekyll and Mr Hyde*

STAGE 5 • 1800 HEADWORDS
... future continuous – future perfect –
passive (modals, continuous forms) –
would have conditional clauses – modals + perfect infinitive ...

If he had spoken Estella's name, I would have hit him. I was so
angry with him, and so depressed about my future, that I could
not eat the breakfast. Instead I went straight to the old house.
Great Expectations

STAGE 6 • 2500 HEADWORDS
... passive (infinitives, gerunds) – advanced modal meanings –
clauses of concession, condition

When I stepped up to the piano, I was confident. It was as if I
knew that the prodigy side of me really did exist. And when I
started to play, I was so caught up in how lovely I looked that
I didn't worry how I would sound. *The Joy Luck Club*

BOOKWORMS · FANTASY & HORROR · STAGE 2

The Mystery of Allegra

PETER FOREMAN

Allegra is an unusual name. It means 'happy' in Italian, but the little girl in this story is sometimes very sad. She is only five years old, but she tells Adrian, her new friend, that she is going to die soon. How does she know?

And who is the other Allegra? The girl in a long white nightdress, who has golden hair and big blue eyes. The girl who comes only at night, and whose hands and face are cold, so cold . . .

BOOKWORMS · FANTASY & HORROR · STAGE 2

Voodoo Island

MICHAEL DUCKWORTH

Mr James Conway wants to make money. He wants to build new houses and shops – and he wants to build them on an old graveyard, on the island of Haiti.

There is only one old man who still visits the graveyard; and Mr Conway is not afraid of one old man.

But the old man has friends – friends in the graveyard, friends who lie dead, under the ground. And when Mr Conway starts to build his houses, he makes the terrible mistake of disturbing the sleep of the dead . . .